We're riding on a caravan to places far away.

A year ago we left Xi'an, the summer sun was bright.
We tugged our camels to their feet and tied the cargo tight.
We paused beneath the city gate and heard the Tower Bell.
Before we took the Silk Road west, we stopped to wave farewell.

We're riding on a caravan, a bumpy, humpy caravan,

Written by Laurie Krebs   Illustrated by Helen Cann

We're riding on a caravan, a bumpy, humpy caravan,

We're riding on a caravan to places far away.

Nine months ago we reached Lanzhou, as leaves began to fall.
We crossed the Yellow River and drew near the city wall.
We traded silk for bags of wool. We liked its pleasant smell.
We bought fresh fruit and vegetables to eat and take to sell.

We're riding on a caravan, a bumpy, humpy caravan,

We're riding on a caravan to places far away.

Six months ago we reached Dunhuang. A brisk wind chilled the air.
Around the lush oasis there were sand dunes everywhere.
We sold some silk and precious stones. We traded rice for bread.
We filled our jugs with water for the desert road ahead.

We're riding on a caravan, a bumpy, humpy caravan,

We're riding on a caravan to places far away.

Five months ago we reached Hami, worn out and sick and cold.
For winter in the desert was as harsh as we'd been told.
We warmed ourselves with goat-head soup and steaming cups of tea,
And rested there for several days before we left Hami.

We're riding on a caravan, a bumpy, humpy caravan,

We're riding on a caravan to places far away.

Three months ago we reached Turpan and felt the touch of spring.
We passed fresh fields and vineyards that were just awakening.
We stopped to trade at mud-brick huts where grapes were hung to dry,
To turn into the raisins that the caravans would buy.

We're riding on a caravan, a bumpy, humpy caravan,

We're riding on a caravan to places far away.

A week ago, we reached Kashgar. Our journey's end was near,
For it was summer once again and we'd been gone a year.
Our bodies were exhausted and the camels' feet were sore.
The trip along the Silk Road was two thousand miles or more!

We're stopping with our caravan, our humpy, bumpy caravan,

We're stopping with our caravan, and for a while we'll stay.

Hooray! Today is market day, the reason that we came.
For Kashgar's Sunday market is of legendary fame.
The people at this great bazaar, each from a different land,
Are speaking many languages that we don't understand.

But everyone has gathered here to buy or sell or trade,
Replenishing their caravans with purchases they've made.
We'll sell the silk that we have brought till every bolt is gone,
Then buy exotic merchandise to take back to Xi'an.

There's ivory from India and curry spice and teas,
And carpets from the Middle East and woven tapestries.
And horses from Arabia and flocks of goats and sheep,
And hairy yaks from mountain towns, where snow and ice pile deep.

We're loading up our caravan, our humpy, bumpy caravan,

Too soon the sun is setting and the market shutters down.
The caravans are piled high, preparing to leave town.
For some will make the journey through the mountains to the west,
And some will take the southern route because they know it best.

We're loading up our caravan, for home is far away.

But we will travel to the east. We've done it all before.
We'll travel on the Silk Road till we reach Xi'an once more.

KYRGYZSTAN

Ysyk Köl

HAMI

Tian Shan Mountains

TURPAN

DUNHUANG

KASHGAR

Taklamakan
Desert

Lake
Nor

Karakoram
Mountains

N

W · E

S

TIBET

Himalayan Mountains

INDIA

MONGOLIA
Gobi Desert
The Great Wall of China
Bohai Sea
Sunwei Mountains
LANZHOU
XI'AN
The Yellow River
CHINA

The Story of Silk

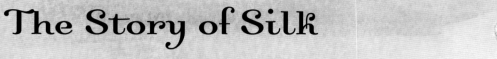

It all began with a young Chinese empress, a little worm and a big secret…

In ancient times, so the story goes, the Chinese emperor's new bride, Hsi Ling-shi, was sitting in her garden beneath a mulberry tree. A cocoon fell from above into her cup of hot tea, and as she drew it from the water, it unwound into a long, delicate thread of silk.

From this accident, the Chinese discovered how to form thread from the cocoons of silkworm moths. Hundreds of tiny worms (actually caterpillars) hatched from the moths' eggs. For six weeks they feasted night and day on mulberry leaves until they were large enough to spin cocoons.

The cocoons were gathered by workers, who softened them with steam or hot air. Unwinding several cocoons at a time, they carefully twisted the fine strands into silk thread. Then the thread was woven into cloth and dyed in many different vibrant hues.

The finished fabric was strong and airy and beautiful. It made brilliant flags and banners for the Chinese armies. People from far away were fascinated by the silk and wanted to make it for themselves. The Chinese were much too clever to share their secret, however. The preparation of silk was carefully guarded, and for a long time no one else knew how it was made.

Today many countries other than China produce silk, and machines have taken over much of the work. But the story truly began a long time ago with a young empress, a little worm and a big secret.

The History of the Silk Road

The caravan path known as the Silk Road is thousands of years old. Historians think the long, long path was the first trade route between the peoples of the East and the West.

Europeans loved Chinese silk and were eager to buy it. So caravans, laden with fabric, would travel west through mountain kingdoms and desert villages to deliver it. But silk was not their only cargo. The Chinese also carried furs, spices, metals, jade, ceramics and lacquerware. On their way, they stopped at oases and trading posts to sell their goods, barter for new things and buy water and supplies. At the same time, caravans going east from Europe brought gems, gold, silver, ivory, tapestries and perfume to Asia.

Very few caravans made the entire trip along the Silk Road. It was much too long! Usually caravans would stop at a place where people could rest. New drivers and fresh animals would continue the journey. Often the people returned home, but sometimes they stayed to raise their families in the new village. This way, different groups of people came to live along the Silk Road. They brought with them new religions and art, new languages and inventions and, best of all, new ideas.

China's Silk Road is only part of the ancient caravan path. One route continued west from Kashgar through the mountains to Samarkand and Central Asia. Another followed the southern route through mountain passes into India. The Silk Road even reached all the way to Europe! Today many of the Chinese oases mentioned in this story are bustling cities, just as they must have been centuries ago.

One of the most famous explorers who passed along the Silk Road was Italian merchant Marco Polo. Almost eight hundred years ago, he journeyed between Italy and China, a trip that took several years. We are lucky to have his stories that tell us about people he met and the things he saw as he made his way along the ancient Silk Road.

Places Along the Chinese Silk Road

Xi'an (shee-*ahn*)

The ancient city of Xi'an was the starting point for caravans heading west along the Silk Road. Located in the fertile valleys of the Wei and Yellow Rivers, Xi'an's old city walls and gates, pagodas and bell towers still exist amidst the city's modern buildings. The famous Terracotta Warriors, said to have guarded the tomb of an early emperor (221–210 BCE), were uncovered in 1974, making Xi'an a popular tourist and archaeological site today.

Lanzhou (lahn-*joe*)

Lanzhou, the capital of Ganzu province, was an important caravan stop along the Silk Road. More than 300 miles (483km) west of Xi'an and nestled in a narrow valley between barren hills, Lanzhou's mild climate and location along the Yellow River made it a useful link between Tibet, Mongolia and other parts of China. Goods were shipped along the river on rafts of inflated animal hide, and with the cargo came new people, who settled among the Han Chinese.

Dunhuang (*dun*-hwong)

Over 600 miles (965km) from Lanzhou, at the end of China's Great Wall, lay another principal trading post, Dunhuang. Caravan drivers from both the east and west stopped to replenish their supplies and give thanks for safe passage through the dangerous country. The Mogao Caves, which house a treasure trove of Buddhist manuscripts, wall paintings and sculpture, reflect the visitors' gratitude as well as their hope for continued safety.

Hami (hah-*mee*)

Hami, set below sea level, more than 200 miles (322km) from Dunhuang, was the next major stop on the Silk Road. Its diverse population includes a number of minority groups such as the Hui, Kazakhs, Mongols and Uygurs in addition to the Han Chinese. Hami is famous for its sweet melons, which were a popular item of trade for the caravans. The oasis borders the Taklamakan Desert, which means "go in and never come out" and which was a hazard for people on the Silk Road.

Turpan (tuhr-*pan*)

Over 200 miles (322km) past Hami was the oasis of Turpan, another significant caravan stop. Like Hami, it rests below sea level, experiences extreme temperature changes and is dominated by the Taklamakan Desert. However, karez channels, an underground water system fed by streams from the Flaming Mountains, irrigate lush fields and vineyards. White raisins, the area's most famous crop, have been dried in clay buildings and sold in markets for centuries.

Kashgar (kash-*gahr*)

The fabled city of Kashgar was the last oasis on China's Silk Road, nearly 750 miles (1,207km) from Turpan and close to the country's western border. Here, at the foot of the Pamir Mountains, at the juncture of China's northern and southern caravan routes, weary visitors found rest and fresh supplies. Kashgar's Sunday market, still in existence, remains a melting pot of cultures and languages, religions and traditions, reflecting the varied faces of China.

Author's Note

My husband and I started taking trips around the world after our children graduated from college. I've been lucky enough to visit many different countries over six continents, including an unforgettable tour of China along the Silk Road. We began our journey from Xi'an and went west along the northern route to the Afghan border, with Dr. Albert Dien, a professor of Chinese from Stanford University, as our guide and translator.

We went by plane, bus, van, boat, donkey cart and even camel! On one bus trip through the desert, we found ourselves in a dust storm. Sand swirled and the sky darkened. I could imagine how people in the ancient days might have lost their way.

We stayed in hotels and inns along the way, and sampled many interesting foods. We loved Mongolian hot pot — very spicy broths that ranged from hot to mouth-numbing. We dipped meat or fish into the broths to cook. We also tried camel paw!

We saw gorgeous sights that inspired the words and images in this book. We visited a grape farm in Turpan, where grapes are dried into raisins in clay houses. The houses have square air holes that help the fruit dry quickly in the dry desert climate. I was surprised by the size of the oases we visited, where thousands of people live in lush cities surrounded by mountains of sand.

The markets along the Silk Road are full of interesting sights — and smells! I remember the earthy scent of stews, and woks of fried rice and noodles, kebabs and dumplings. I wondered at the huge vats of soup, pots of bubbling duck feet and piles of crunchy, beady-eyed whole fish. The smell of bread drew me to the clay ovens where heaps of bagel-like rolls and a flatbread called naan were baked.

The most memorable experience on our trip was visiting the Kashgar market. People still travel from all over and gather at the Sunday market to buy, barter and sell goods. There were donkey carts everywhere filled with cabbage, tomatoes, figs, eggs, parsnips and greens. Sheep and goats were lined up neatly along a fence, waiting to be sold. Buyers checked the teeth of donkeys and horses, examined their hoofs and patted every part of their body before haggling over the price. I was drawn to the beautiful silks, which I chose to bring home as souvenirs.

For centuries, the Silk Road has allowed people from many countries and cultures to meet and mingle and share. As an author of books for children about people all over the world, I'm inspired by this sharing of cultures. I'm fascinated by all the ways children are alike even when their languages and lifestyles differ. I love to bring my readers along on my travels through my books.

— Laurie Krebs

All photographs by Bill Krebs

To Dee and Don, with love
— L. K.

For Charlotte Welply —
keep journeying, with much love
— H. C.

Barefoot Books
2067 Massachusetts Ave
Cambridge, MA 02140

Barefoot Books
29/30 Fitzroy Square
London, W1T 6LQ

First published in Great Britain by Barefoot Books, Ltd and in the United States of America
by Barefoot Books, Inc in 2005 as *We're Riding on a Caravan: An Adventure on the Silk Road*
This paperback edition first published in 2017

Graphic design by Louise Millar, London, and Barefoot Books
Edited and art directed by Emma Parkin, Barefoot Books
Reproduction by Grafiscan, Verona
Printed in China on 100% acid-free paper
This book was typeset in Adobe Caslon Pro, Dalliance and Octavian
The illustrations were prepared in watercolour, graphite and collage on 140lb Bockingford paper

ISBN 978-1-78285-344-2
British Cataloguing-in-Publication Data:
a catalogue record for this book is available from the British Library

Library of Congress Cataloging-in-Publication Data
is available under LCCN 2004028591

1 3 5 7 9 8 6 4 2